A·WORLD·OF
FLOWER·FAIRIES

A·WORLD·OF FLOWER·FAIRIES

Poems and pictures by

CICELY MARY BARKER

◆

FREDERICK WARNE

*The reproductions in this book have been made using the most modern
electronic scanning methods from entirely new transparencies of Cicely
Mary Barker's original watercolours. They enable Cicely Mary Barker's skill
as an artist to be appreciated as never before.*

The original illustrations of the Celandine Fairy, the Dog-Violet Fairy,
the Primrose Fairy, the Bluebell Fairy, the Speedwell Fairy, the Cowslip Fairy,
the Heart's-Ease Fairy and the Snowdrop Fairy have been lost so a first edition
has been used to reproduce these pictures.

FREDERICK WARNE

Published by the Penguin Group
27 Wrights Lane, London W8 5TZ, England
Penguin Books USA Inc., 375 Hudson Street, New York, New York 10014, USA
Penguin Books Australia Ltd, Ringwood, Victoria, Australia
Penguin Books Canada Ltd, 10 Alcorn Avenue, Toronto, Ontario M4V 3B2
Penguin Books (NZ) Ltd, 182-190 Wairau Road, Auckland 10, New Zealand

Penguin Books Ltd, Registered Offices: Harmondsworth, Middlesex, England

First published in this format 1992

5 7 9 10 8 6 4

ISBN 0 7232 4002 7

Colour reproduction by Anglia Graphics Ltd, Bedford
Printed and bound in Great Britain by
William Clowes Limited, Beccles and London

✦CONTENTS✦

The Celandine Fairy

The Celandine Fairy

◆ THE SONG OF ◆
THE CELANDINE FAIRY

Before the hawthorn leaves unfold,
Or buttercups put forth their gold,
By every sunny footpath shine
The stars of Lesser Celandine.

◆ THE SONG OF ◆
THE DOG-VIOLET FAIRY

The wren and robin hop around;
   The Primrose-maids my neighbours be;
The sun has warmed the mossy ground;
Where Spring has come, I too am found:
   The Cuckoo's call has wakened me!

The Dog-Violet Fairy

The Primrose Fairy.

The Primrose Fairy

◆ THE SONG OF ◆
THE PRIMROSE FAIRY

The Primrose opens wide in spring;
  Her scent is sweet and good:
It smells of every happy thing
  In sunny lane and wood.
I have not half the skill to sing
  And praise her as I should.

She's dear to folk throughout the land;
  In her is nothing mean:
She freely spreads on every hand
  Her petals pale and clean.
And though she's neither proud nor grand,
  She is the Country Queen.

◆ THE SONG OF ◆
THE BLUEBELL FAIRY

My hundred thousand bells of blue,
   The splendour of the Spring,
They carpet all the woods anew
With royalty of sapphire hue;
The Primrose is the Queen, 'tis true.
    But surely I am King!
      Ah yes,
    The peerless Woodland King!

Loud, loud the thrushes sing their song;
   The bluebell woods are wide;
My stems are tall and straight and strong;
From ugly streets the children throng,
They gather armfuls, great and long,
    Then home they troop in pride—
      Ah yes,
    With laughter and with pride!

(This is the Wild Hyacinth. The Bluebell of Scotland
is the Harebell.)

The Bluebell Fairy

The Speedwell Fairy

♦ THE SONG OF ♦
THE SPEEDWELL FAIRY

Clear blue are the skies;
   My petals are blue;
   As beautiful, too,
As bluest of eyes.

The heavens are high:
   By the field-path I grow
   Where wayfarers go,
And "Good speed," say I;

"See, here is a prize
   Of wonderful worth:
   A weed of the earth,
As blue as the skies!"

(There are many kinds of Speedwell: this is the Germander.)

◆ THE SONG OF ◆
THE COWSLIP FAIRY

The land is full of happy birds
And flocks of sheep and grazing herds.

I hear the songs of larks that fly
Above me in the breezy sky.

I hear the little lambkins bleat;
My honey-scent is rich and sweet.

Beneath the sun I dance and play
In April and in merry May.

The grass is green as green can be;
The children shout at sight of me.

The Cowslip Fairy

The Heart's-Ease Fairy

◆ THE SONG OF ◆
THE HEART'S-EASE FAIRY

Like the richest velvet
   (I've heard the fairies tell)
Grow the handsome pansies
   within the garden wall;
When you praise their beauty,
   remember me as well—
Think of little Heart's-ease,
   the brother of them all!

Come away and seek me
   when the year is young,
Through the open ploughlands
   beyond the garden wall;
Many names are pretty
   and many songs are sung:
Mine—because I'm Heart's-ease—
   are prettiest of all!

(An old lady says that when she was a little girl the children's
name for the Heart's-ease or Wild Pansy was Jump-up-and-
kiss-me!)

◆ THE SONG OF ◆
THE POPPY FAIRY

The green wheat's a-growing,
  The lark sings on high;
In scarlet silk a-glowing,
  Here stand I.

The wheat's turning yellow,
  Ripening for sheaves;
I hear the little fellow
  Who scares the bird-thieves.

Now the harvest's ended,
  The wheat-field is bare;
But still, red and splendid,
  I am there.

The Poppy Fairy

The Bird's-Foot Trefoil Fairy

◆ THE SONG OF ◆
THE BIRD'S-FOOT TREFOIL FAIRY

Here I dance in a dress like flames,
And laugh to think of my comical names.
Hoppetty hop, with nimble legs!
Some folks call me *Bacon and Eggs*!
While other people, it's really true,
Tell me I'm *Cuckoo's Stockings* too!
Over the hill I skip and prance;
I'm *Lady's Slipper,* and so I dance,
Not like a lady, grand and proud,
But to the grasshoppers' chirping loud.
My pods are shaped like a dicky's toes:
That is what *Bird's-Foot Trefoil* shows;
This is my name which grown-ups use,
But children may call me what they choose.

◆ THE SONG OF ◆
THE NIGHTSHADE FAIRY

My name is Nightshade, also Bittersweet;
    Ah, little folk, be wise!
Hide you your hands behind you when we meet,
    Turn you away your eyes.
My flowers you shall not pick, nor berries eat,
    For in them poison lies.

(Though this is so poisonous, it is not the Deadly Nightshade,
but the Woody Nightshade. The berries turn red a little later on.)

The Nightshade Fairy

The Heather Fairy

◆ THE SONG OF ◆
THE HEATHER FAIRY

"Ho, Heather, ho! From south to north
Spread now your royal purple forth!
Ho, jolly one! From east to west,
The moorland waiteth to be dressed!"

I come, I come! With footsteps sure
I run to clothe the waiting moor;
From heath to heath I leap and stride
To fling my bounty far and wide.

(The heather in the picture is bell heather, or heath; it is
different from the common heather which is also called ling.)

◆ THE SONG OF ◆
THE SCARLET PIMPERNEL FAIRY

By the furrowed fields I lie,
Calling to the passers-by:
"If the weather you would tell,
Look at Scarlet Pimpernel."

When the day is warm and fine,
I unfold these flowers of mine;
Ah, but you must look for rain
When I shut them up again!

Weather-glasses on the walls
Hang in wealthy people's halls:
Though I lie where cart-wheels pass
I'm the Poor Man's Weather-Glass!

The Scarlet Pimpernel Fairy

The Greater Knapweed Fairy

◆ THE SONG OF ◆
THE GREATER KNAPWEED FAIRY

Oh, please, little children, take note of my
    name:
To call me a thistle is really a shame:
I'm harmless old Knapweed, who grows
    on the chalk,
I never will prick you when out for your
    walk.

Yet I should be sorry, yes, sorry indeed,
To cut your small fingers and cause them
    to bleed;
So bid me Good Morning when out for
    your walk,
And mind how you pull at my very tough
    stalk.

(Sometimes this Knapweed is called Hardhead; and he has a
brother, the little Knapweed, whose flower is not quite like this.)

◆ THE SONG OF ◆
THE ROSE FAIRY

Best and dearest flower that grows,
Perfect both to see and smell;
Words can never, never tell
Half the beauty of a Rose—
Buds that open to disclose
Fold on fold of purest white,
Lovely pink, or red that glows
Deep, sweet-scented. What delight
 To be Fairy of the Rose!

The Rose Fairy

The Michaelmas Daisy Fairy

◆ THE SONG OF ◆
THE MICHAELMAS DAISY FAIRY

"Red Admiral, Red Admiral,
   I'm glad to see you here,
     Alighting on my daisies one by one!
I hope you like their flavour
   and although the Autumn's near,
     Are happy as you sit there in the sun?"

"I thank you very kindly, sir!
   Your daisies *are* so nice,
     So pretty and so plentiful are they;
The flavour of their honey, sir,
   it really does entice;
     I'd like to bring my brothers, if I may!"

"Friend butterfly, friend butterfly,
   go fetch them one and all!
     I'm waiting here to welcome every guest;
And tell them it is Michaelmas,
   and soon the leaves will fall,
     But *I* think Autumn sunshine is the best!"

◆ THE SONG OF ◆
THE WAYFARING TREE FAIRY

My shoots are tipped with buds as dusty-grey
As ancient pilgrims toiling on their way.

Like Thursday's child with far to go, I stand,
All ready for the road to Fairyland;

With hood, and bag, and shoes, my name to suit,
And in my hand my gorgeous-tinted fruit.

The Wayfaring Tree Fairy

The Robin's Pincushion Fairy

◆ THE SONG OF ◆
THE ROBIN'S PINCUSHION FAIRY

People come and look at me,
Asking who this rogue may be?
—Up to mischief, they suppose,
Perched upon the briar-rose.

I am nothing else at all
But a fuzzy-wuzzy ball,
Like a little bunch of flame;
I will tell you how I came:

First there came a naughty fly,
Pricked the rose, and made her cry;
Out I popped to see about it;
This is true, so do not doubt it!

◆ THE SONG OF ◆
THE ACORN FAIRY

To English folk the mighty oak
   Is England's noblest tree;
Its hard-grained wood is strong and good
   As English hearts can be.
And would you know how oak-trees grow,
   The secret may be told:
You do but need to plant for seed
   One acorn in the mould;
For even so, long years ago,
   Were born the oaks of old.

The Acorn Fairy

The Black Bryony Fairy

◆ THE SONG OF ◆
THE BLACK BRYONY FAIRY

Bright and wild and beautiful
For the Autumn festival,
I will hang from tree to tree
Wreaths and ropes of Bryony,
To the glory and the praise
Of the sweet September days.

(There is nothing black to be seen about this Bryony, but
people do say it has a black root; and this may be true, but you
would need to dig it up to find out. It used to be thought a cure
for freckles.)

◆ THE SONG OF ◆
THE BLACKBERRY FAIRY

My berries cluster black and thick
For rich and poor alike to pick.

I'll tear your dress, and cling, and tease,
And scratch your hands and arms and knees.

I'll stain your fingers and your face,
And then I'll laugh at your disgrace.

But when the bramble-jelly's made,
You'll find your trouble well repaid.

The Blackberry Fairy

The Rose Hip Fairy

✦ THE SONG OF ✦
THE ROSE HIP FAIRY

Cool dewy morning,
  Blue sky at noon,
White mist at evening,
  And large yellow moon;

Blackberries juicy
  For staining of lips;
And scarlet, O scarlet
  The Wild Rose Hips!

Gay as a gipsy
  All Autumn long,
Here on the hedge-top
  This is my song.

◆ THE SONG OF ◆
THE WHITE BRYONY FAIRY

Have you seen at Autumn-time
    Fairy-folk adorning
All the hedge with necklaces,
    Early in the morning?
Green beads and red beads
    Threaded on a vine:
Is there any handiwork
    Prettier than mine?

(This Bryony has other names—White Vine, Wild Vine, and
Red-berried Bryony. It has tendrils to climb with, which Black
Bryony has not, and its leaves and berries are quite different.
They say its root is white, as the other's is black.)

The White Bryony Fairy

The Beechnut Fairy

◆ THE SONG OF ◆
THE BEECHNUT FAIRY

O the great and happy Beech,
  Glorious and tall!
Changing with the changing months,
  Lovely in them all:

Lovely in the leafless time,
  Lovelier in green;
Loveliest with golden leaves
  And the sky between,

When the nuts are falling fast,
  Thrown by little me—
Tiny things to patter down
  From a forest tree!

(You may eat these.)

◆ THE SONG OF ◆
THE SNOWDROP FAIRY

Deep sleeps the Winter,
    Cold, wet, and grey;
Surely all the world is dead;
    Spring is far away.
Wait! the world shall waken;
    It is not dead, for lo,
The Fair Maids of February
    Stand in the snow!

The Snowdrop Fairy

The Spindle Berry Fairy

◆ THE SONG OF ◆
THE SPINDLE BERRY FAIRY

See the rosy-berried Spindle
All to sunset colours turning,
Till the thicket seems to kindle,
Just as though the trees were burning.
While my berries split and show
Orange-coloured seeds aglow,
One by one my leaves must fall:
Soon the wind will take them all.
Soon must fairies shut their eyes
For the Winter's hushabies;
But, before the Autumn goes,
Spindle turns to flame and rose!

◆ THE SONG OF ◆
THE PLANE TREE FAIRY

You will not find him in the wood,
    Nor in the country lane;
But in the city's parks and streets
    You'll see the Plane.

O turn your eyes from pavements grey,
    And look you up instead,
To where the Plane tree's pretty balls
    Hang overhead!

When he has shed his golden leaves,
    His balls will yet remain,
To deck the tree until the Spring
    Comes back again!

The Plane Tree Fairy

The Box Tree Fairy

◆ THE SONG OF ◆
THE BOX TREE FAIRY

Have you seen the Box unclipped,
Never shaped and never snipped?
Often it's a garden hedge,
Just a narrow little edge;
Or in funny shapes it's cut,
And it's very pretty; *but*—

But, unclipped, it is a tree,
Growing as it likes to be;
And it has its blossoms too;
Tiny buds, the Winter through,
Wait to open in the Spring
In a scented yellow ring.

And among its leaves there play
Little blue-tits, brisk and gay.

◆ THE SONG OF ◆
THE OLD-MAN'S-BEARD FAIRY

This is where the little elves
Cuddle down to hide themselves;
Into fluffy beds they creep,
Say good-night, and go to sleep.

(Old-Man's-Beard is Wild Clematis; its flowers are called
Traveller's Joy. This silky fluff belongs to the seeds.)

The Old-Man's-Beard Fairy

The Blackthorn Fairy

◆ THE SONG OF ◆
THE BLACKTHORN FAIRY

The wind is cold, the Spring seems long
    a-waking;
  The woods are brown and bare;
Yet this is March: soon April will be making
  All things most sweet and fair.

See, even now, in hedge and thicket tangled,
    One brave and cheering sight:
The leafless branches of the Blackthorn,
    spangled
  With starry blossoms white!

(The cold days of March are sometimes called "Blackthorn
Winter".)

◆ THE SONG OF ◆
THE WINTER ACONITE FAIRY

Deep in the earth
I woke, I stirred.
I said: "Was that the Spring I heard?
For something called!"
"No, no," they said;
"Go back to sleep. Go back to bed.

"You're far too soon;
The world's too cold
For you, so small." So I was told.
But how could I
Go back to sleep?
I could not wait; I had to peep!

Up, up, I climbed,
And here am I.
How wide the earth! How great the sky!
O wintry world,
See me, awake!
Spring calls, and comes; 'tis no mistake.

The Winter Aconite Fairy

The Christmas Tree Fairy

◆ THE SONG OF ◆
THE CHRISTMAS TREE FAIRY

The little Christmas Tree was born
   And dwelt in open air;
It did not guess how bright a dress
   Some day its boughs would wear;
Brown cones were all, it thought, a tall
   And grown-up Fir would bear.

O little Fir! Your forest home
   Is far and far away;
And here indoors these boughs of yours
   With coloured balls are gay,
With candle-light, and tinsel bright,
   For this is Christmas Day!

A dolly-fairy stands on top,
   Till children sleep; then she
(A live one now!) from bough to bough
   Goes gliding silently.
O magic sight, this joyous night!
   O laden, sparkling tree!

◆ THE SONG OF ◆
THE ROSE-BAY
WILLOW-HERB FAIRY

On the breeze my fluff is blown;
So my airy seeds are sown.

Where the earth is burnt and sad,
I will come to make it glad.

All forlorn and ruined places,
All neglected empty spaces,

I can cover—only think!—
With a mass of rosy pink.

Burst then, seed-pods; breezes, blow!
Far and wide my seeds shall go!

(Another name for this Willow-Herb is "Fireweed",
because of its way of growing where there have
been heath or forest fires.)

The Rose-Bay Willow-Herb Fairy

The Red Clover Fairy

◆ THE SONG OF ◆
THE RED CLOVER FAIRY

The Fairy: O, what a great big bee
Has come to visit me!
He's come to find my honey.
O, what a great big bee!

The Bee: O, what a great big Clover!
I'll search it well, all over,
And gather all its honey.
O, what a great big Clover!

◆ THE SONG OF ◆
THE TANSY FAIRY

In busy kitchens, in olden days,
Tansy was used in a score of ways;
Chopped and pounded,
   when cooks would make
Tansy puddings and tansy cake,
Tansy posset, or tansy tea;
Physic or flavouring tansy'd be.
       People who know
       Have told me so!

That is my tale of the past; today,
Still I'm here by the King's Highway,
Where the air from the fields
   is fresh and sweet,
With my fine-cut leaves and my flowers neat.
Were ever such button-like flowers seen—
Yellow, for elfin coats of green?
       Three in a row—
       I stitch them so!

The Tansy Fairy

The Agrimony Fairies

◆ THE SONG OF ◆
THE AGRIMONY FAIRIES

Spikes of yellow flowers,
    All along the lane;
When the petals vanish,
    Burrs of red remain.

First the spike of flowers,
    Then the spike of burrs;
Carry them like soldiers,
    Smartly, little sirs!

◆ THE SONG OF ◆
THE ALMOND BLOSSOM FAIRY

Joy! the Winter's nearly gone!
Soon will Spring come dancing on;
And, before her, here dance I,
Pink like sunrise in the sky.
Other lovely things will follow;
Soon will cuckoo come, and swallow;
Birds will sing and buds will burst,
But the Almond is the first!

The Almond Blossom Fairy

The Pear Blossom Fairy

◆ THE SONG OF ◆
THE PEAR BLOSSOM FAIRY

Sing, sing, sing, you blackbirds!
   Sing, you beautiful thrush!
It's Spring, Spring, Spring; so sing, sing, sing,
   From dawn till the stars say "hush".

See, see, see the blossom
   On the Pear Tree shining white!
It will fall like snow, but the pears will grow
   For people's and birds' delight.

Build, build, build, you chaffinch;
   Build, you robin and wren,
A safe warm nest where your eggs may rest;
   Then sit, sit, sit, little hen!

◆ THE SONG OF ◆
THE LILAC FAIRY

White May is flowering,
   Red May beside;
Laburnum is showering
   Gold far and wide;
But *I* sing of Lilac,
   The dearly-loved Lilac,
Lilac, in Maytime
   A joy and a pride!

I love her so much
   That I never can tell
If she's sweeter to look at,
   Or sweeter to smell.

The Lilac Fairy

The Beech Tree Fairy

◆ THE SONG OF ◆
THE BEECH TREE FAIRY

The trunks of Beeches are smooth and grey,
    Like tall straight pillars of stone
In great Cathedrals where people pray;
    Yet from tiny things they've grown.
About their roots is the moss; and wide
    Their branches spread, and high;
It seems to us, on the earth who bide,
    That their heads are in the sky.

And when Spring is here,
  and their leaves appear,
    With a silky fringe on each,
Nothing is seen so new and green
    As the new young green of Beech.
O the great grey Beech is young, is young,
    When, dangling soft and small,
Round balls of bloom from its twigs are hung,
    And the sun shines over all.

◆ THE SONG OF ◆
THE GUELDER ROSE FAIRIES

There are two little trees:
In the garden there grows
The one with the snowballs;
All children love *those*!

The other small tree
Not everyone knows,
With her blossoms spread flat—
Yet they're both Guelder Rose!

But the garden Guelder has nothing
When her beautiful balls are shed;
While in Autumn her wild little sister
Bears berries of ruby red!

The Guelder Rose Fairies

The Elder Fairy

◆ THE SONG OF ◆
THE ELDER FAIRY

When the days have grown in length,
When the sun has greater power,
Shining in his noonday strength;
When the Elder Tree's in flower;
When each shady kind of place
By the stream and up the lane,
Shows its mass of creamy lace—
Summer's really come again!

◆ THE SONG OF ◆
THE CHERRY TREE FAIRY

Cherries, a treat for the blackbirds;
    Cherries for girls and boys;
And there's never an elf in the treetops
    But cherries are what he enjoys!

Cherries in garden and orchard,
    Ripe and red in the sun;
And the merriest elf in the treetops
    Is the fortunate Cherry-tree one!

The Cherry Tree Fairy

The Poplar Fairy

◆ THE SONG OF ◆
THE POPLAR FAIRY

White fluff is drifting like snow round our feet;
    Puff! it goes blowing
    Away down the street.

Where does it come from? Look up and see!
    There, from the Poplar!
    Yes, from that tree!

Tassels of silky white fluffiness there
    Hang among leaves
    All a-shake in the air.

Fairies, you well may guess, use it to stuff
    Pillows and cushions,
    And play with it—puff!

(This is called the Black Poplar; but only, I think, because
there is also a White Poplar, which has white leaves. The
very tall thin Poplar is the Lombardy.)

◆ THE SONG OF ◆
THE ELM TREE FAIRY

Soft and brown in Winter-time,
Dark and green in Summer's prime,
All their leaves a yellow haze
In the pleasant Autumn days—
See the lines of Elm trees stand
Keeping watch through all the land
Over lanes, and crops, and cows,
And the fields where Dobbin ploughs.
All day long, with listening ears,
Sits the Elm-tree Elf, and hears
Distant bell, and bleat, and bark,
Whistling boy, and singing lark.
Often on the topmost boughs
Many a rook has built a house;
Evening comes; and overhead,
Cawing, home they fly to bed.

The Elm Tree Fairy

The Scilla Fairy

◆ THE SONG OF ◆
THE SCILLA FAIRY

"Scilla, Scilla, tell me true,
Why are you so very blue?"

Oh, I really cannot say
Why I'm made this lovely way!

I might know, if I were wise.
Yet—I've heard of seas and skies,

Where the blue is deeper far
Than our skies of Springtime are.

P'r'aps I'm here to let you see
What that Summer blue will be.

When you see it, think of me!

◆ THE SONG OF ◆
THE FORGET-ME-NOT FAIRY

Where do fairy babies lie
Till they're old enough to fly?
Here's a likely place, I think,
'Mid these flowers, blue and pink,
(Pink for girls and blue for boys:
Pretty things for babies' toys!)
Let us peep now, gently. Why,
Fairy baby, here you lie!

Kicking there, with no one by,
Baby dear, how good you lie!
All alone, but O, you're not—
You could *never* be—forgot!
O how glad I am I've found you,
With Forget-me-nots around you,
Blue, the colour of the sky!
Fairy baby, Hushaby!

The Forget-me-not Fairy

The Tulip Fairy

◆ THE SONG OF ◆
THE TULIP FAIRY

Our stalks are very straight and tall,
    Our colours clear and bright;
Too many-hued to name them all—
    Red, yellow, pink, or white.

And some are splashed, and some, maybe,
    As dark as any plum.
From tulip-fields across the sea
    To England did we come.

We were a peaceful country's pride,
    And Holland is its name.
Now in your gardens we abide—
    And aren't you glad we came?

(But long, long ago, tulips were brought from Persian
gardens, before there were any in Holland.)

◆ THE SONG OF ◆
THE PINK FAIRIES

Early in the mornings,
   when children still are sleeping,
Or late, late at night-time,
   beneath the summer moon,
What are they doing,
   the busy fairy people?
Could you creep to spy them,
   in silent magic shoon,

You might learn a secret,
   among the garden borders,
Something never guessed at,
   that no one knows or thinks:
Snip, snip, snip, go busy fairy scissors,
Pinking out the edges
   of the petals of the Pinks!

Pink Pinks, white Pinks,
   double Pinks, and single,—
Look at them and see
   if it's not the truth I tell!
Why call them Pinks
   if they weren't pinked out by *someone*?
And what but fairy scissors
   could pink them out so well?

The Pink Fairies

The Snapdragon Fairy

◆ THE SONG OF ◆
THE SNAPDRAGON FAIRY

Into the Dragon's mouth he goes;
    Never afraid is he!
There's honey within for him, he knows,
    Clever old Bumble Bee!
The mouth snaps tight; he is lost to sight—
    How will he ever get out?
He's doing it backwards—nimbly too,
    Though he is somewhat stout!

Off to another mouth he goes;
    Never a rest has he;
He must fill his honey-bag full, he knows—
    Busy old Bumble Bee!
And Snapdragon's name is only a game—
    It isn't as fierce as it sounds;
The Snapdragon Elf is pleased as Punch
    When Bumble comes on his rounds!

◆ THE SONG OF ◆
THE LAVENDER FAIRY

"Lavender's blue, diddle diddle"—
  So goes the song;
All round her bush, diddle diddle,
  Butterflies throng;
(They love her well, diddle diddle,
  So do the bees;)
While she herself, diddle diddle,
  Sways in the breeze!

"Lavender's blue, diddle diddle,
  Lavender's green";
She'll scent the clothes, diddle diddle,
  Put away clean—
Clean from the wash, diddle diddle,
  Hanky and sheet;
Lavender's spikes, diddle diddle,
  Make them all sweet!

(The word "blue" was often used in old days where
 we should say "purple" or "mauve".)

The Lavender Fairy

The Heliotrope Fairy

◆ THE SONG OF ◆
THE HELIOTROPE FAIRY

Heliotrope's my name; and why
People call me "Cherry Pie",
That I really do not know;
But perhaps they call me so,
'Cause I give them such a treat,
Just like something nice to eat.
For my scent—O come and smell it!
How can words describe or tell it?
And my buds and flowers, see,
Soft and rich and velvety—
Deepest purple first, that fades
To the palest lilac shades.
Well-beloved, I know, am I—
Heliotrope, or Cherry Pie!

◆ THE SONG OF ◆
THE MARIGOLD FAIRY

Great Sun above me in the sky,
So golden, glorious, and high,
My petals, see, are golden too;
They shine, but cannot shine like you.

I scatter many seeds around;
And where they fall upon the ground,
More Marigolds will spring, more flowers
To open wide in sunny hours.

It is because I love you so,
I turn to watch you as you go;
Without your light, no joy could be.
Look down, great Sun, and shine on me!

The Marigold Fairy

B

Bugle

The Bugle Fairy

◆ THE SONG OF ◆
THE BUGLE FAIRY

At the edge of the woodland
Where good fairies dwell,
Stands, on the look-out,
A brave sentinel.

At the call of his bugle
Out the elves run,
Ready for anything,
Danger, or fun,
Hunting, or warfare,
By moonshine or sun.

With bluebells and campions
The woodlands are gay,
Where bronzy-leaved Bugle
Keeps watch night and day.

◆ THE SONG OF ◆
THE DOUBLE DAISY FAIRY

Dahlias and Delphiniums,
  you're too tall for me;
Isn't there a *little* flower
  I can choose for D?

In the smallest flower-bed
Double Daisy lifts his head,
With a smile to greet the sun,
You, and me, and everyone.

Crimson Daisy, now I see
You're the little lad for me!

Double Daisy

The Double Daisy Fairy

Gorse

G

The Gorse Fairies

◆ THE SONG OF ◆
THE GORSE FAIRIES

"When gorse is out of blossom,"
   (Its prickles bare of gold)
"Then kissing's out of fashion,"
   Said country-folk of old.
Now Gorse is in its glory
   In May when skies are blue,
But when its time is over,
   Whatever shall we do?

O dreary would the world be,
   With everyone grown cold—
Forlorn as prickly bushes
   Without their fairy gold!
But this will never happen:
   At every time of year
You'll find one bit of blossom—-
   A kiss from someone dear!

◆ THE SONG OF ◆
THE LILY-OF-THE-VALLEY FAIRY

Gentle fairies, hush your singing:
Can you hear my white bells ringing,
Ringing as from far away?
Who can tell me what they say?

Little snowy bells out-springing
From the stem and softly ringing—
Tell they of a country where
Everything is good and fair?

Lovely, lovely things for L!
Lilac, Lavender as well;
And, more sweet than rhyming tells,
Lily-of-the-Valley's bells.

(Lily-of-the-Valley is sometimes called Ladders to Heaven.)

Lily-of-the-Valley

The Lily-of-the-Valley Fairy

Queen of the Meadow

The Queen of the Meadow Fairy

◆ THE SONG OF ◆
THE QUEEN OF THE MEADOW FAIRY

Queen of the Meadow
  where small streams are flowing,
What is your kingdom
  and whom do you rule?
"Mine are the places
  where wet grass is growing,
Mine are the people
  of marshland and pool.

"Kingfisher-courtiers,
  swift-flashing, beautiful,
Dragon-flies, minnows,
  are mine one and all;
Little frog-servants who
  wait round me, dutiful,
Hop on my errands
  and come when I call."

Gentle Queen Meadowsweet,
  served with such loyalty,
Have you no crown then,
  no jewels to wear?
"Nothing I need
  for a sign of my royalty,
Nothing at all
  but my own fluffy hair!"

◆ THE SONG OF ◆
THE STRAWBERRY FAIRY

A flower for S!
Is Sunflower he?
He's handsome, yes,
But what of me?—

In my party suit
Of red and white,
And a gift of fruit
For the feast tonight:

Strawberries small
And wild and sweet,
For the Queen and all
Of her Court to eat!

S

Strawberry

The Strawberry Fairy

Wallflower

The Wallflower Fairy

◆ THE SONG OF ◆
THE WALLFLOWER FAIRY

Wallflower, Wallflower, up on the wall,
Who sowed your seed there?
                    "No one at all:
Long, long ago it was blown by the breeze
To the crannies of walls
    where I live as I please.

"Garden walls, castle walls, mossy and old,
These are my dwellings;
    from these I behold
The changes of years;
    yet, each spring that goes by,
Unchanged in my sweet-smelling
    velvet am I!"

◆ THE SONG OF ◆
THE ZINNIA FAIRY

Z for Zinnias, pink or red;
See them in the flower-bed,
Copper, orange, all aglow,
Making such a stately show.

I, their fairy, say Good-bye,
For the last of all am I.
Now the Alphabet is said
All the way from A to Z.

The Zinnia Fairy